Tea Time!

By Andrew Davenport

Copyright © 2019 Moon and Me

Scholastic Children's Books,
Euston House, 24 Eversholt Street,
London NW1 1DB, UK

A division of Scholastic Ltd
London ~ New York ~ Toronto ~ Sydney ~ Auckland
Mexico City ~ New Delhi ~ Hong Kong

Published in the UK by Scholastic Ltd, 2019

ISBN 978 1407 18853 9

Printed and bound in Italy

2 4 6 8 10 9 7 5 3 1

MIX
Paper from
responsible sources
FSC® C023419
FSC
www.fsc.org

www.scholastic.co.uk

Moon, can we have a story?

"A story? What a good idea!"

Once upon a time, there was a magical toy that came to life whenever the moon shone. Hello, Pepi Nana!

Pepi Nana wrote a letter to the moon.

Tiddle toddle,
Please come to tea,
and we can have a story.
Yours, lovingly out of
the window,
Pepi Nana

Away went the tiny letter to the moon.

Pepi Nana didn't know that on the moon lived Moon Baby.

Moon Baby opened Pepi Nana's letter. He wanted to visit Pepi Nana, very much.

Moon Baby picked up his magical kalimba, put on his yellow gloves, and pulled up his hood. Off he flew, to visit Pepi Nana.

The Toy House!

"**Where is Pepi Nana?**" thought Moon Baby.
So, he rang the doorbell. *Ding dong!*

"Tiddle toddle!" said Pepi Nana.
"Moon Baby has come to visit!"

Time to wake up the toys!

Moon Baby played his magical kalimba.
And one by one, the toys woke up.

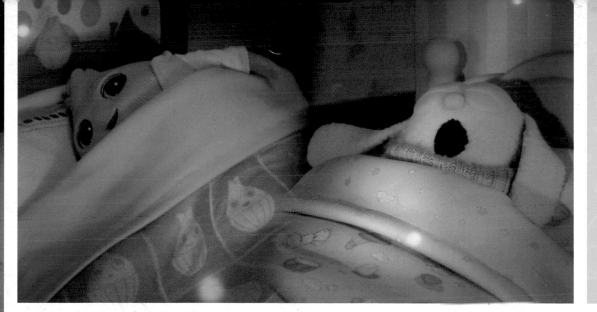

Hello, Mr Onion.
"Onions!"

Hello, Dibillo.
"Yawn!"

Hello, Little Nana.
"Poop-poop!"

Hello, Lambkin.
"Baa!"

Hello, Colly Wobble.
"Tinkle-tinkle!"

Hello, Lily Plant.
"Oh, my dears!"

Inside the little Toy House, everybody was very busy.
Mr Onion chose a book to read.

But when he went to sit in his
chair, he saw something new.
"Onions!"

"Paper crowns!" said Mr Onion.

Pepi Nana and Little Nana tried the crowns on.

"**Oh my dears!**" said Lily Plant. "**You look like princesses!**"

Pepi Nana said, "**Tiddle toddle! What a useful thing for a story!**"

Moon Baby plays a magical tune on his kalimba to take us to Storyland.

Hold hands!

Once upon a time there was a Little Princess, living in a Little Castle.

One day, the Little Princess looked out of her little window.

"Today I will visit the Big Princess in her Big Castle," she said.

So, off she went with her best friend Lambkin, to visit the Big Castle where the Big Princess lived.

"**Poop-poop!**" said the Little Princess.
"**What a Big Castle!**"

"**I've come to visit the Big Princess,**" said the Little Princess.

Mr Onion blew on his trumpet.
Toot! Toot!

"**Come in, come in!**" said the Big Princess. "**It's tea time!**"

The Little Princess had
tea with the Big Princess.

"What a big cake!"
said the Little Princess.
"Poop-poop!"

"**Thank you very much for tea!**" said the Little Princess.
"**Thank you very much for visiting!**"
said the Big Princess.

Visiting, visiting,
Yes, yes, yes!
I'm going visiting a
Big Princess!

Visiting, visiting,
You and me
Sit together – let's have tea!

Now we know a happy way
To be together every day!

Visiting is so much fun —
If I could, I would visit everyone!

The Toy House!

"**Oh, my dears!**" said Lily Plant.
"**Just in time for tea!**"

"**Tea time, again!**" said Little Nana.

"**Tea time is our favourite time!**" said Pepi Nana.

And everybody thought she was right about that.

"Hush, hush," says the Moon, "It's time to go to sleep."

Goodnight, Toy House friends! Goodnight, Pepi Nana! Goodnight, Moon Baby!